The Plane Crash

The Plane Crash

발   행 | 2024년 03월 01일
저   자 | 연지훈, Jihoon Yeon
펴낸이 | 한건희
펴낸곳 | 주식회사 부크크
출판사등록 | 2014.07.15.(제2014-16호)
주   소 | 서울특별시 금천구 가산디지털1로 119 SK트윈타워 A동 305호
전   화 | 1670-8316
이메일 | info@bookk.co.kr

ISBN | 979-11-410-7259-9

www.bookk.co.kr

The Plane Crash

Jihoon Yeon

CONTENT

Chapter 1. The Plane Crash   6

Chapter 2. Isolated Island   10

Chapter 3. The Start of An Adventure   15

Chapter 4. The Light   21

Chapter 5. Who Are You?   26

Chapter 6. Poison Ivy   31

Chapter 7. The God   35

Chapter 8. The First Message   39

Chapter 9. The Second Message   44

Chapter 10. At Home At Last   48

"The Plane Crash," crafted solely by Jihoon Yeon, is an imaginative tale depicting the journey of a family stranded in Guam after a plane crash, as they search for two crucial messages for their escape. This novel is filled with gripping scenarios and tense moments as the family bravely ventures through the unknown island, facing various challenges and dangers. Readers will embark on an adventure with the family, learning about the importance of courage and hope in the journey of survival. "The Plane Crash" promises an exploration into a new world brimming with excitement and wonder.

Chapter 1
The Plane Crash

We were on the plane to Guam.

"I should take a nap,"

said my younger sister.

I had nothing to do.

This was the first time in my twelve miserable years going out of the country because of my fear of plane crashes and my fear of heights.

I heard that the plane would take off one hour late because of the bad weather, but for some reason, one hour felt like one second because of my worries.

Now the plane is really going. I held my breath and waited.

We went through the runway as we went forward and forward. And then finally we went off.

After a few seconds, the plane was going at the speed of light, and it went into the air like that. I went to sleep.

But, Three hours after takeoff, the plane started to shake.

My mom said,
"It's because of the air."

But I knew it wasn't. The lights went off and on and then off again.

I could hear the sound of the engine falling away, and then the plane splashed in the water.

I heard a BOOM.

After that, I didn't hear, see, or smell anything.

Chapter 2
Isolated island

As I opened my eyes, I could see an isolated island out the plane's window.

My little sister and my mom had their eyes closed.

As I stood up in the aisle and looked around, I saw our plane had crashed and we were floating on the water.

Nearby, I saw an island, so I woke up my mom and little sister.

Together, we jumped off the plane into the water and we swam to the island.

We wrote SOS in the sand, but nobody could see us.

After an hour, we just gave up.

My leg hurt because of the crash. I could smell something weird too.

As I looked back, I could see a weird figure.

Thump, Thump, Thump!

A giant horse was galloping toward me. I am right-handed, like a normal 12-year-old.

So I grabbed a stick with my right hand and ran as fast as I could.

Then the horse stopped, and I put it in the horse's eye. Then I made a knife.

It was hard, but after a few hundred seconds, I did it.

Then I put it in the horse's heart, and it died.

For lunch, we made a small fire and put the horse on a spit.

And also, we found some mangos and rice floating in the water.

"Horse meat is better than I thought," my young sister said.

"Yeah," my mom said.

So from that day on, we started to live like this, until one day we were making a fire, then there was a poof, and the fire grew giant.

We did all we could do to stop it.

Then the fire's color was turning super red.

Chapter 3
The Start of An Adventure

After the fire, I went on a walk to see the damage, and I saw something strange.

There was a cave behind a giant rock.

I called my mom and little sister, and we pushed the rock as hard as we could.

Finally, we could go inside the cave, but as we went in, the rock moved and blocked the cave again.

"No!!"

We went deeper in the cave, and deeper and deeper. Then we heard a small noise.

"Beep, beep, beep, beep.
1 hour left. "

I looked around. A bomb was ticking.

I told my mom and my little sister to run as fast as they could and I followed them.

I looked at my watch that I found in the crash.

It was at 5:30.

We saw the bomb at 5:15.
So "only 45 minutes," I thought.

"30 minutes,
15 minutes,
5 minutes,
1 minute. "

There were 10 seconds to 6:15.

10, 9, 8, 7, 6, 5, 4, 3, 2,1....

We then jumped as far as we could.

BOOM!!!!

We were safe.

But if we were about 3 seconds later, we could have been dead. Nearby a little fox got killed.

We were happy we were alive, but we were so sleepy and hungry.

All we could find was a broken cracker in my pocket.

We each ate about 2g and went to sleep.

When we woke up,
I asked my mom and sister,
"What dream did you have ? "

They said they had a dream about living here for 10 years.

"I also had that dream," I said.
"Oh no. Maybe that might be real," my little sister said.

"If we ran long enough, maybe this long cave would have an end," my mom said.

We decided to try it, so we ran and
ran and ran and ran.

I thought we ran about 500 km, but
there was still no end.

Chapter 4
The Light

When we were walking, I saw a weird light in the wall of the cave.

I told my mom and little sister to come, and we looked closer.

It was a small hole outside.

We crawled in and looked down.

"Ah!" I screamed because it was so high and I have a fear of heights.

It was so scary.

After an hour, we finally went out of the cave. We were so happy to be free in this world. But the bad thing is that the light outside didn't look like sunlight.

It looked much stranger and much deeper.

I was so curious about the light, so I made a small string, put my watch on it, and coded it to take a picture every hour.

About a day later, I looked at my watch, and there were 24 mysterious pictures. And all of them had worm soup, a bright light, and some parrot soup.

That meant there may have been a person living in the cave. I might be a bad person, because I thought about whether to help him or not.

After 3 hours, I decided to just leave him there to live a bad life or whatever.

"It's better with fewer people." I thought.

So I didn't help him.

But then, at night, I heard a sound.

"Please help me. Please help me. Please help me."

I said, "I can't do anything else."

But I made a super-long rope and put it down.
He climbed up.

"What's your name?" I asked.
"My name is Max," he said.

"How old are you?"
"About 37,000 years old."

I was so surprised that I asked again.
He said it again.

"37,000 years old, for real?" I asked.

"Yes, I was born in America, but when
I was on an airplane, it crashed, and I
lived here for 31,000 years."

Chapter 5
Who Are You?

My eyes were as big as the moon.
I didn't believe what I just heard.

I told both my little sister and my
mom. And they were the same.

I wanted to investigate him more. So every day I talked to Max.

I learned that Max was a scientist and made a medicine that will make him never die.

Then, when he went on a trip to Guam, his plane crashed. But because he never dies, he didn't die.

At night, I could see Max doing something weird.

As I got closer, I spied on him. And he began to form slowly into a wolf and became black.

He didn't just get black, he also became bigger.

I got the giant sword and blocked him. Then, I shook the sword rapidly.

"STOP!!"

"I am Max," he said.

"Well, now you are not. And you're immortal anyway," I said.

"I am sorry, but that was just a lie to trick you."

"Okay." Like that, I made a fire and tricked him to go into it.

Then, I woke my mom and we ate him.

"Was Max a wolf?" my little sister asked.

"Yes, he was," I said.

"But he was so kind to us."

"That was only because he was tricking us."

"Ugh," my little sister said.

"Why?" I asked.

"I don't think we should EAT wolf meat.

It tastes bad and also smells bad.

And I think I could taste a rock inside, and it is very different from cow meat," my little sister said.

"Yeah, I think that too," my mom said.

"It is better than not eating," I said.

Then, we stood up but then, my sister said, "OW!" my sister said.

"Why?" I asked.

"Something is so scratchy in my leg,"
she said.

"Maybe it is poison IVY," I said.

"POISON IVY!!!!!!!!

I don't want my leg to be poisoned,"
she said.

'It' s okay. It is not as poisonous as you
think," I said.

But her leg did not look good.

Chapter 6
Poison Ivy

The next day and the day after that,
I could see my sister's leg getting more
gray.

And my sister asked, "Do you think it

will really be okay?"

"Yes, oh, no." I said.

"What?" my little sister said.

"I will do all I can to help you, but don't walk any more."

Then we went to the broken plane, and then we found some medicine to give her, and we gave her it.

Every day, it didn't get better but only got worse.

One day when my sister woke up, her leg was black.

It got blacker and blacker and blacker.

So she couldn't move it for dinner.
We found a strawberry in the field, so
we ate it together, splitting it into
thirds.

But because of my sister's injury, she
couldn't move, so we needed to find
more strawberries.

There was only one strawberry.

But then I had an idea. I got water
from the sea, and I put it in my
sister's leg.

"OW!" my sister said,

but then as her leg became whiter
and whiter, it became almost my skin
color.

"Now it's better." ,I thought.

"I didn't know that seawater would do this stuff. Maybe seawater is more useful than I thought."

Chapter 7
The God

When I went inside the sea, I could
see something weird.

All my scars and injuries got better.

The seawater had powers of healing.

But that was not all.

I could hear something.

"Find two messages and put them here."

"Who are you?" I asked.

I touched everywhere, but the only thing I could feel was water and sand.

"I am the God of Poseidon. "

I couldn't believe it.

"Now, could God be real?"

I asked myself.

I told my little sister and mom and they were happy that they could finally leave the isolated island.

They thanked me for going inside the ocean.

"Where could these two messages be?", my little sister asked.
"I don't know," I said.
"It could be anywhere," my mom said.
"Let's eat something first." I said.

We looked everywhere. In the cave we eventually found an old musty tea bag.

"Aw," my little sister said.
"We could make a cup of tea." I said.

So we made a cup of tea.
"Yeah, it's better than I thought," my little sister said.

After we drank the tea, we made a plan.

Chapter 8
The First Message

The plan was to look everywhere. First, me and then my little sister, then my mom.

When it was my turn, I could only find

a bottle in the sand.

Next, when my little sister came, she couldn't find anything.

But when my mom came, she found many things.

At dinner time, we looked for the message in my mom's pile.

But there was no message.

After that, we forgot about the message stuff for a while and just lived like that for about one week.

There was a lot of stuff happening. I lost my watch, and also the poison ivy thing happened to me.

But then one night, when we were eating dinner, a mysterious thing happened.

When I was looking inside the bottle, I could see something inside. Then I opened it.

It said,

"To the person who finds this.

I know it is hard to live on an isolated island. Don't worry if you find only one more message on this island. You will get out of the island. "

"YES!"

I finally found the first message.

"What?!" my mom said.

"Yay," my little sister said.

"I've saved this in my pocket for years," I said, "but let's eat some almonds and chocolate chips to party."

I threw a few almonds and chocolate chips in my mouth.

"Mmm, Yummy! "

My little sister ate some too.

"That' s good!"

"Yeah, do you have more?" mom asked.

"No!"

"Aw man~!" my sister said.

"That was so good, I want to eat more."

"Me too," Mom said.

"Let's find the second message," I said.

Chapter 9
The Second Message

We were looking for a message when we heard something.

Beep, Beep.

Beep,Beep.

"Is that a bomb sound?" my little
sister asked.

"Yeah, it is," I said.

"RUN!"

We ran and ran for a while, but it
wasn't a bomb.

We returned to where we'd heard
the sound. And we dug in the sand.

I could see a small Apple watch.
Then I had an idea.

I picked up the watch, and then
looked inside the app messages.

There were no messages.

So I waited for one.

I finally got a message about a week later.

"Yay, we got the second message!" we said.

But nothing happened.

"That's weird," I said.

"Oh, I didn't get the first message."

So I got the first message.

"You finally found the two messages. Come here tomorrow exactly at 3:30 p.m," the god of Poseidon said.

"How do we know it's 3:30 p.m. without a watch?" my little sister said.

"I don't know."

"Should we make one?" I asked,

"But we have a watch," my little sister said.

"Oh" I said.

It said it was at 3:30pm.

Then, I went to the place with my mom and little sister.

Chapter 10
At Home At Last

'Will this really happen? Will I really go home?' I thought.

Then I closed my eyes and waited.

And then, at last, there was power in my legs and with the speed of light, we flew in the sky.

It was so beautiful, a yellowish and whitish sky blue.

But the problem is that we needed to be in the sky all day.

After four days, I saw my home.

'Wow, now I'm dropping at a murderous speed.'

And then, finally, I was at home.

It was weird being at home.

Everything was so easy to do.

I didn't need to look for food in the refrigerator. There's so much.

"Where is dad?" I asked.

"Maybe he's gone to work," my little sister said.

"Maybe he's looking for us," my mom said.

"Let's eat first; I'm so hungry!"
So we ate.

After we ate, I walked outside and felt the grass under my feet. I looked for my yellow cat. I looked and looked.

Finally, I found him fighting with my pet dog.

I pulled a toothpick out of my pocket to clean between my teeth, and I watched them.

It was so interesting.

So I forgot to stop them from getting hurt.

But when the cat squeaked, I stopped them.

Then my dad came outside and asked me, "What happened to you?"

And I said,

"It's a long story."

Congratulations on the publication of your first novel, Jihoon!

We, your loving parents, are bursting with pride for your dedication and passion.

May this book be the first step in your journey of life, and know that we'll always be here to support you as you reach for even greater dreams.
We love you, Jihoon!

Mar 1st, 2024
Mom & Dad